GREAT MOMENTS IN
OLYMPIC SOCCER

BY THOMAS CAROTHERS

SUPER SOCCER

SportsZone

An Imprint of Abdo Publishing
abdobooks.com

abdobooks.com

Published by Abdo Publishing, a division of ABDO, PO Box 398166, Minneapolis, Minnesota 55439. Copyright © 2019 by Abdo Consulting Group, Inc. International copyrights reserved in all countries. No part of this book may be reproduced in any form without written permission from the publisher. SportsZone™ is a trademark and logo of Abdo Publishing.

Printed in the United States of America, North Mankato, Minnesota
092018
012019

THIS BOOK CONTAINS
RECYCLED MATERIALS

Cover Photos: David Klein/AP Images, (foreground); Shutterstock Images, (ball)
Interior Photos: Shutterstock Images, 1; David E. Klutho/Sports Illustrated/Getty Images, 4–5; Nuccio Dinuzzo/KRT/Newscom, 6; ullstein bild Dtl./Getty Images, 9; AP Images, 11; Chris O'Meara/AP Images, 12–13; David Cannon/Getty Images, 15; Luca Bruno/AP Images, 17; Ricardo Mazalan/AP Images, 19; Stephane Mantey/Corbis Sport/Getty Images, 20; Scott Barbour/Getty Images Sport/Getty Images, 22–23; Joe Ledford/KRT/Newscom, 24; Robert Cianflone/FIFA/Getty Images, 27; Nic Bothma/Epa/Rex Features, 28

Editor: Bradley Cole
Series Designer: Laura Polzin

Library of Congress Control Number: 2018949091

Publisher's Cataloging-in-Publication Data

Names: Carothers, Thomas, author.
Title: Great moments in Olympic soccer / by Thomas Carothers.
Description: Minneapolis, Minnesota : Abdo Publishing, 2019 | Series: Super soccer | Includes online resources and index.
Identifiers: ISBN 9781532117442 (lib. bdg.) | ISBN 9781641856263 (pbk) | ISBN 9781532170300 (ebook)
Subjects: LCSH: Olympic games--Juvenile literature. | Soccer--Juvenile literature. | Soccer players--Juvenile literature.
Classification: DDC 796.3346--dc23

★TABLE OF★ CONTENTS

CHAPTER 1

USA WINS FIRST WOMEN'S GOLD

A young Team USA just survived the group stage of the first-ever women's Olympic soccer tournament. They advanced to play Norway in a tense semifinal match. Norway took the lead 18 minutes into the match. The Americans couldn't manage to score in the game until Michele Akers's goal in the 76th minute. Time ran out with the countries still tied 1–1, but a US midfielder burned the Norwegian goalkeeper in extra time for the 2–1 win.

The eight countries that competed in soccer in the 1996 Olympics included the United States and China. Team USA had won 2–0 over China in the 1995 Women's World Cup to finish third. At the 1996 Olympics, the teams played to a scoreless tie in their group game. China went on to finish atop the group.

Mia Hamm fights for the ball versus Norway's Gro Espeseth in the 1996 Olympic semifinal.

Mia Hamm (9) was a force in American soccer in the 1990s.

China defeated Brazil 3–2 in their semifinal game. Now the two teams that played for third place the year before would face off for the Olympic gold medal.

Team USA and China took the field in front of more than 76,000 fans. Most of them were clad in red, white, and blue at the University of Georgia's football stadium. At the time it was the largest crowd ever to watch a women's sporting event.

The stadium erupted as US midfielder Shannon MacMillan scored the game's first goal. It happened in the 19th minute when she pounced on a rebound after teammate Mia Hamm's shot hit the post. Chinese midfielder Sun Wen answered quickly just 13 minutes later, bringing China even at 1–1.

The score remained tied until midway through the second half. In the 68th minute, US defender Joy Fawcett got behind the Chinese defense with the ball. She passed to Tiffeny Milbrett. Milbrett chipped the ball into the back of the net and celebrated with a somersault.

Milbrett's goal put Team USA up 2–1. The record crowd held its breath. The Americans played hard to fend off their rivals for the final 20-plus minutes. And they held on to win the first women's Olympic gold medal.

The excitement generated by the tournament proved that women's soccer was there to stay at the Olympics. The pioneering women in that first tournament set the stage for many more thrilling Olympic competitions to come.

WOMEN'S SOCCER BAN

Women's soccer had been banned over 70 years earlier in several European countries, including England. Countries started lifting bans in the 1970, but women's professional soccer took time to return to its previous popularity. The 1995 Women's World Cup was organized by FIFA in response to the sport's growth.

CHAPTER 2

POLAND COMPLETES A LONG JOURNEY

The 1972 Olympic Games in Munich represented the end of a long journey for the Polish men's soccer team. Thirty-six years earlier in Berlin, Poland recorded an upset victory over Great Britain on its way to a fourth-place finish during the 1936 Olympics. Those games were played under the watch of Adolf Hitler in the capital city of Nazi Germany.

Three years later, Hitler and the Nazis invaded Poland to begin World War II. The nation of Poland temporarily ceased to exist. While the Nazis were later defeated, and Poland was restored as a country, the nation did not compete in Olympic soccer again until 1952.

In Olympic competition, Poland struggled. The Polish men lost in the first round of the 1952 Olympics and did not qualify

A player from the Poland team, *left*, battles a German opponent in the 1936 Olympics.

for the tournament in 1956. After winning one game and losing twice in 1960, Poland failed to qualify again until 1972.

The 1972 Munich Olympics were the first time the games were held in Germany since 1936. This was also a high point of Polish soccer history, as the team had surpassed all of their previous attempts in international play.

Poland won five games and drew once, outscoring its opponents by 15 goals to earn a spot in the gold-medal game against Hungary. Poland was led by the tournament's top scorer, midfielder Kazimierz Deyna. He would make his mark in the championship game.

Hungary took a 1–0 lead with a goal just three minutes before halftime. However, Deyna would not allow his team to lose. Just two minutes into the second half, he shrugged off a pair of defenders and launched a long strike into the Hungarian goal to tie the score at 1–1.

In the 68th minute, Deyna answered the call for Poland one last time. After a flurry in front of the Hungary goal, he tucked the ball in between a diving goalkeeper and the near post for his ninth goal of the tournament. Poland took the lead 2–1.

Polish players celebrate after winning gold over Hungary.

Adoring teammates mobbed Deyna in front of 80,000 fans at the Olympic Stadium in Munich. Twenty-two minutes later, after a final Hungarian corner kick was turned away, the final whistle blew to announce that Poland was atop the soccer world as Olympic champions.

Polish players hugged one another while others lifted their arms in triumph. After a 36-year detour between Berlin and Munich, Poland had completed its journey at last. The victory kicked off a run of success for Poland. The team took third in the 1974 World Cup and finished second to East Germany in the 1976 Olympics. But no feat has ever topped Poland's Olympic gold in 1972.

CHAPTER 3

NIGERIA WINS FIRST SOCCER GOLD FOR AFRICA

Since the first competition in 1900, men's Olympic soccer has been dominated by Europe and South America. Aside from a gold medal won by Canada in 1904, the top of the medal stand was occupied by a European or South American team in every Olympics. That was until 1996.

Nigeria was not a long shot entering the 1996 Atlanta Games. The Nigerians were well thought of in soccer. Many figured that when Africa did claim its first Olympic gold, Nigeria would be the country to win it. The only question was when.

The Nigerians were placed in Group D. They needed to finish first or second in the group to advance to the quarterfinals. But joining Nigeria in Group D was Brazil, a world power in soccer.

Jay-Jay Okocha (10) of Nigeria fends off Japan's Teruyoshi Ito during group play.

Nigeria beat Hungary and Japan and advanced despite losing to Brazil 1–0 in the group finale.

After beating Mexico in the quarterfinals, Nigeria got a rematch with Brazil. In glitzy fashion, Brazil scored the first four goals of a spirited, high-tempo game. More than 78,000 fans watched Brazil quickly take the lead. Fortunately for Nigeria, one of those scores was an own goal. Brazilian defender Roberto Carlos put the ball into his own net. Nigerian forward Tijani Babangida had tried to score from the left side, but his kick had been too wide. Carlos then tried to clear the ball away from the Brazilian goal but kicked it into the net instead.

Nigeria refused to give up despite trailing 3–1 heading into the late stages of the game. After intercepting the ball at midfield, forward Victor Ikpeba scored on a 20-yard screamer into the lower corner. That cut Brazil's lead to 3–2 in the 78th minute.

Heading into the final minute of regulation, Brazil was still clinging to its one-goal lead. That was until captain Nwankwo Kanu found the ball in front of the Brazil goal off a throw-in.

Emmanuel Amunike, *left*, celebrates Nigeria's gold medal after scoring the winning goal against Argentina.

was left wide open and tapped the ball easily past goalkeeper Pablo Cavallero for the game winner.

It was a gold medal win not only for Nigeria but for all of Africa. The entire continent celebrated the victory. Nigeria became just the second team not from Europe or South America to win an Olympic gold. But the world would have to wait only four more years for another team to join that exclusive group.

CHAPTER 4

CAMEROON WINS GOLD

It took 96 years for Nigeria to win Africa's first gold medal in Olympic soccer. African soccer fans only needed to wait a mere four years to claim a second gold. Cameroon stood atop the podium at the very next Olympic games.

The Cameroonians began the Olympic tournament in Australia by winning their first group game, defeating Kuwait 3–2 in the opener. From there, the future gold medalists managed just a pair of draws against the United States and the Czech Republic to finish up group play. The results may not have been ideal, but they were enough to advance to the knockout stage. There Cameroon impressed the world.

Cameroon was not scared of Brazil heading into the quarterfinal match. Forward Patrick M'Boma scored first on a

Cameroon took down world power Brazil 2–1 to advance to the semifinals.

free kick to put Cameroon up 1–0 just 17 minutes into the game. Brazil tied the game at 1–1 before the final whistle to send the game into extra time. Brazil missed on several chances to score the golden goal. Midfielder Modeste M'bami won the game for Cameroon instead. M'bami blasted home a goal from the top of the penalty box with six minutes left in the second extra session to win it 2–1 for Cameroon.

Next up for Cameroon was formidable Chile. The game was scoreless through the first 77 minutes. Then Cameroonian defender Patrice Abanda put the ball into his own net to give Chile a 1–0 lead. Cameroon had to fight hard, but M'Boma scored in the 84th minute to tie the game.

Cameroon's Patrick M'Boma attacks the Spanish defense with a header in the finals.

The game remained tied for five more minutes before M'Boma was taken down inside the penalty box. Cameroon was awarded a penalty kick for the foul. Defender Lauren Bisan Etamé-Mayer was chosen to take the kick. Bisan Etamé-Mayer kicked right and the keeper lunged left, and Cameroon advanced into the Olympic final with a 2–1 win.

Awaiting Cameroon in the final was the heavily favored Spanish squad. The thrilling matchup played out in front of more than 104,000 fans at the Olympic Stadium in Sydney.

Spain scored just two minutes into the game and doubled its lead before halftime. But Cameroon got a ray of hope as Spanish defender Iván Amaya scored an own goal to make the score 2–1. Forward Samuel Eto'o tapped home a cross by M'Boma five minutes later to make the score 2–2. Neither team managed to score again through the rest of regulation and extra time. The game went to penalty kicks.

Amaya missed his penalty kick for Spain. Cameroon made its first four kicks. Spain made its next four kicks. Cameroon clinched the gold medal with its final penalty kick by Pierre Womé. Africa had won back-to-back Olympic gold medals.

CHAPTER 5

NORWAY TAKES GOLD FROM USA

Cameroon was not the only team to win its first Olympic soccer gold in the 2000 Sydney Olympics. Norway's women made it to the top of the medal stand for the first time at the Sydney Olympics.

The rivalry between Norway and the United States helped fuel women's soccer during the 1990s. They battled for golds at the highest levels of the sport while women's soccer was starting to gain momentum around the world.

The two opened the Olympic tournament against one another. But it wasn't the start that Norway wanted. Team USA scored twice early in a 2–0 win. But the Norwegians did not let the shutout get them down. Norway and the United States both qualified for the knockout round.

Norway's Goeril Kringen, *right*, fends off a German defender in the semifinals.

Norway's win over rival Team USA finally secured an Olympic gold medal for its women's soccer team.

Norway won its semifinal game in a most unusual fashion. The Norwegians did not even score. German defender Tina Wunderlich headed the ball into her own goal. Meanwhile, Team USA beat Brazil 1–0 to move on to the finals.

It wasn't looking like the Norwegians' year in the final as Team USA once again scored an early goal. Forward Tiffeny Milbrett put the Americans up 1–0 five minutes into the game. Team USA was dreaming of a second straight gold medal.

But the Norwegians scored twice to take the lead. Defender Gro Espeseth headed home a corner kick just before halftime. The Norwegians had tied the score against their rivals.

Despite being outshot, Norway stunned the Americans with a go-ahead goal in the 78th minute. The Norwegians took the lead as forward Ragnhild Gulbrandsen fought off a pair of defenders to head the ball into the net before being tackled by her happy teammates. But the 2–1 lead was not safe. Milbrett struck again on a header in the final moments of regulation time to tie the game. Norway had more work to do.

Yet, the night belonged to Norway. Despite dominating possession for most of the game, Team USA gave up the golden goal 11 minutes into extra time. A long midfield pass bounced off the head of defender Joy Fawcett in front of the American goal. The ball fell to forward Dagny Mellgren, who beat two defenders and slipped the ball past US goalkeeper Siri Mullinix.

The victory set off a wave of celebration and relief among the Norwegians, who had temporarily halted the growth of the American soccer empire.

US-NORWAY RIVALRY

The US loss to Norway in the 2000 Olympic gold medal game marked just the second time that Team USA had been defeated in Olympic or Women's World Cup play. Both of the losses came against Norway.

CHAPTER 6

TEAM USA DEFEATS NEW RIVAL FOR GOLD

In 2011 Japan defeated the United States on penalty kicks to win its first Women's World Cup. In doing so, Japan found a new rival. The United States was stunned and went into the 2012 London Olympics looking for revenge.

The rematch almost didn't happen because of Canada's arrival on the world stage. Boasting the Olympics' leading scorer, Christine Sinclair, the Canadians nearly recorded a massive upset in the semifinals. Sinclair scored all three goals for Canada. The United States found itself trailing 3–2 in the 73rd minute. A penalty kick goal by American captain Abby Wambach in the 80th minute sent the game into extra time. Team USA won the game in the final seconds of extra time on forward Alex Morgan's header.

Carli Lloyd (10) of Team USA dribbles past a Japanese defender in the gold medal match.

Team USA won its third straight Olympic gold medal at the 2012 London Olympic Games.

The victory set up the rematch the soccer world was hoping to see. The United States faced Japan in front of a record crowd. More than 80,000 fans packed one of the cathedrals of soccer, London's Wembley Stadium.

It was the final Olympic match for Wambach. She had been a big star for Team USA since 2001. But it was her teammate, midfielder Carli Lloyd, who took over the game. Lloyd put the United States up 1–0 after placing a pass from Morgan into the net eight minutes in. Lloyd struck again in the 54th minute. She raced with the ball nearly unchallenged before firing a shot from the top of the penalty box. Lloyd put Team USA up 2–0.

Both teams saw chances to score come and go in a back-and-forth game. Japan broke through at last in the 63rd minute as forward Yūki Ogimi put the ball home following a scramble in front of the US net.

The goal set up a frantic final 30 minutes of play, but the American defense was able to prevent Japan from tying it. With no defenders nearby, goalkeeper Hope Solo turned away Japan's final chance with a diving save.

It was the Americans' third straight Olympic title and fourth overall. The United States and Japan met for another title rematch in the 2015 World Cup, with Team USA winning 5–2 in the final game of Wambach's international tournament career.

INTERNATIONAL SUPERSTAR

Abby Wambach made her first appearance for Team USA in 2001, not long after the loss to Norway in the 2000 Olympic final. By the time her career ended, she was the leading scorer in international soccer with 184 goals. She won two Olympic gold medals and earned her lone World Cup championship with the title win over Japan in 2015.

GLOSSARY

extra time

Two 15-minute periods added to a game if the score is tied at the end of regulation.

formidable

Inspiring fear or respect through strength and power.

forward

Also called a striker, the player who plays nearest the opponent's goal.

goalkeeper

A player whose primary duty is to prevent the ball from entering the net.

golden goal

A goal scored in added extra time to win a game under a sudden death format.

knockout stage

A part of a competition in which one loss eliminates a team.

midfielder

A player who stays mostly in the middle third of the field and links the defenders with the forwards.

own goal

A goal that is accidentally scored by a player against his own team.

penalty kick

A play in which a shooter faces a goalkeeper alone; it is used to decide tie games or as a result of the foul.

pitch

The soccer field.

winger

An attacking midfielder who plays wide.

MORE INFORMATION

BOOKS

Jökulsson, Illugi. *Alex Morgan*. New York: Abbeville Kids, 2015.

Kortemeier, Todd. *Total Soccer*. Minneapolis, MN: Abdo Publishing, 2017.

Marthaler, Jon. *Soccer Trivia*. Minneapolis, MN: Abdo Publishing, 2016.

ONLINE RESOURCES

Booklinks
NONFICTION NETWORK
FREE! ONLINE NONFICTION RESOURCES

To learn more about Olympic soccer, visit **abdobooklinks.com**. These links are routinely monitored and updated to provide the most current information available.

INDEX

ABOUT THE AUTHOR

Thomas Carothers has been a sportswriter for the past 15 years in the Minneapolis–St. Paul area in Minnesota. He has worked for a number of print and online publications, mostly focusing on prep sports coverage. He lives in Minneapolis with his wife and a house full of dogs.